ISBN 978-0-484-43607-6
PIBN 10231216

The Crucifixion
in verse

and

Rhymes of Life

by

James H. Day

———

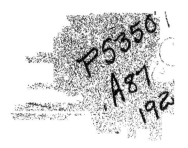

JAMES H. DAY
Author

TO
A FRIEND.

A friend can read one's mind,
And tell what lies behind
*   Your thinking;*
And then will do the deed,
The thing of which you stand in need,
*   Before you ask it.*
One should rather spend eternity
Than just a few days here with thee.
*   Do we see a lesson?*

INDEX

PREFACE

If one heart is soothed, one heart-ache quieted, or, best of all, one inspiration for the better things which lift us above the sordid affairs of every-day life—if that heart finds any of these things in this weak effort, we can but praise the *God* who sends *happiness* our way.

INTERSTATE PRINTING COMPANY
DANVILLE, ILLINOIS

SUNSHINE

Oh! little, little sunbeam,
    How welcome are you here!
You make the dew-drop sparkle
    And to us all give cheer.

Cheer to the sick room,
    Where, on his weary cot
A soldier boy is fighting
    For the life he's got.

For you know you help him
    The disease germs to fight;
In all our sickness,
    We dread to see the night.

Dear little sunbeam,
    You make the children glad;
For since you do your shining,
    The weather isn't bad.

And they can go out playing
    In the bright sunshine,
Each one a-shouting,
    For it's fine, fine, fine!

Dear little children,
    You will grow up soon,
And don't forget your sunshine
    In your afternoon.

Afternoon of life will come,
    But keep this sunbeam thine;
And in this grim old world,
    Your smile will be sunshine.

Sunshine to another,
    Whose path is worry and strife;
And if you hold that little beam,
    You'll have friends for life.

THE CRUCIFIXION

Why do we come to worship Christ,
 All people here tonight?
Because he promised to forgive
 Our sins and give us light.

Light to know what's right or wrong,
 As on our way we go;
This is God's plan for ev'ry one —
 He wishes to have it so.

Way back there when Hebrews reigned,
 They sacrificed each year,
Which only passed them one year more,
 But the sins stood out more clear.

Our sins of nature are punished here—
 We receive the punishment then;—
But the sins of souls are to us unknown—
 That punishment is the dread of men.

But don't forget that Jesus, our Lord,
 Was human over thirty years,
And all of nature's sins he knows—
 He knows the fleshly fears.

And when we reach the great white throne,
 Feeling that we are lost,
There'll be Christ right by that throne—
 He knows, He's borne the cross.

But to get dear Jesus on our side,
 We here on earth must work;
And, like the Lord, the jeers of men
 Be unnoticed; we must not shirk.

Oh! When we think of His last hours,
    The supper and hour of woe,
We feel that surely for such a One
    These punishments can't be so.

He, with His disciples, to the garden went,
    To the garden He went to pray;
Leaving all but three behind, you know,
    He went farther on His way.

And at a point He left the three—
    Peter, James and John.
"Remain and watch," he said to them,
    But they slept when he had gone.

When He returned He found them there,
    All quite fast asleep.
"Could ye not watch with me one hour?"
    But He knew that flesh is weak.

The Saviour knew the hour was at hand.
    Judas betrayed! and he was taken;
Pilate found no guilt in the man,
    But the Jews would not be shaken.

Barrabas, the murderer, they'd rather have
    Than the loving Son of God!
They gave no thought to eternity
    When they'd be under the sod.

The only thing which permitted Rome
    To count His sin at all
Was Pilate saying, "Art king of Jews?"
    "Thou sayest," gave Him His fall.

And then the Roman soldiers so brave—
    Many against God's Son—
Stripped Him to wear a scarlet robe
    And a crown of thorns placed on.

They crushed the crown down over His brow
    And laughed to see the blood flow;
They spit upon his sainted face,
    And would not let Him go.

They laughed and mocked Him everywhere,
    Except a few who tarried,
And going to His bitter cross,
    Which Simon was forced to carry.

Oh! Look upon the feet and hands!
    And bloody face with dust!
Would no one stop them then and there,
    As through the nails were thrust?

Oh! Can't you feel the terrible shock
    As the cross drops into the hole!
No wonder the temple was then shaken;
    No wonder there appeared dead souls.

Darkness then was on the land,
    And people stood in fright.
Listen! What is it Jesus says
    In those shadows, black as night?

"God, forgive them, they know not what
    They do" rings out so-clear;
Christ's dying to save the world;
    Forgiveness is spoken here.

Some gave him vinegar with a sponge,
    When others said, "Let be,
He's dying, and 'twas the Son of God";
    But they never before believed.

Why this suffering and this pain,
    Suffered by God's own Son?
Because through these sufferings great
    Heaven by us may be won.

He's passed through all of this to show
    A way to Heaven; to know
By this one way He's shown us,
    Or we'll never get to go.

He then was buried, as we all know,
    But arose again to life;
He came back to prove it all,
    That He was the Son of Life.

And when the Disciples understood all—
    How holy was their Lord—
They started then to all the world,
    To preach with one accord.

The only way which Christ has given
    Whereby we may begin,
Is to believe, repent, confess,
    Baptized for remission of sin.

And any one not brave enough
    To demonstrate this here
May live a life that's not so bad
    And be lost in the end, I fear.

Christ died upon *Calvary's Cross*
    In suffering to show
Sins may be washed away from you
    As clean as whitest snow.

Baptism doesn't save a man,
    It's only just the beginning;
A *Christian*, he must be from then,
    Or *Heaven* he's not winning.

WHAT CHRISTIANITY HAS ACCOMPLISHED

The Roman empire of the time
    Of which we are speaking
Was ruler of the known world,
    But freedom, some were seeking.

Freedom from this great empire,
    For idols was their belief;
Their haughty sway and tyranny
    Gave some states no relief.

There was ancient Palestine,
    The home of God's own chosen;
But though they were scattered so
    Their belief had not been frozen.

For the law of Moses, sacred was,
    And it warmed every heart;
That some day they would get a King,
    And then Rome must depart.

The Hebrews were a rich old race,
    And some had wandered far;
Their wealth and social works, you know,
    Did not religion bar.

They had it planned, though Rome knew not,
    Just what steps to take;
They'd rise in one mighty mass,
    For this, their new King's sake.

And then there came the tidings glad
    That *Jesus* sure was born;
But they did not shout it to the world,
    Or blow the trumpet's horn.

They knew full well what Rome would do.
　　They would stay at home
Until their *Jesus* started up,
　　And then they'd take all Rome.

Don't you suppose they talked of it,
　　When they would all be free?
For the *Son of God* would then be worth
　　Rome's legions, don't you see?

Imagine their great disappointment,
　　When *Christ* so lowly walked—
He was not clad in armor bright,
　　He merely taught and talked.

Talked to them of a *Kingdom* great
　　Which would be perfect love—
No fighting there, no swords laid bare;
　　But all be as above.

Their faith grew less and less, you know,
　　This was no *King to trust;*
They beat their heads against the wall,
　　Covered their bodies with dust.

How could they great Rome defy
　　When he was not more than
A crazed, jabbering pest, you know,
　　A crazy-minded man?

But one there was believed in *Him*,
　　Besides the twelve selected;
'Twas one of the three wise, wise men,
　　Who knew what was expected.

He knew how God had covenants made
　　With men and people of ages;
To point the way of all to God,
　　Just like the prophets and sages.

He came to divide the worldly things
    From things which are of *Life;*
A life where suffering and sorrow ends,
    Where there will be no strife.

It was so sad—they were so blind
    As not to even believe
When some poor leper was made whole,
    And blind men made to see.

But we all know that Rome would not
    Send *Him* to the cross;
So *His* own people were to blame
    For their own greatest loss.

Then when *He* had arisen,
    Was by *His* disciples heard—
They at last believed on *Him,*
    Believed *His* every word.

We can not tell of all the things
    Which were done to put *Christ* down;
Though many were burned and crucified,
    It made Christianity resound.

Even to Rome was it taken,
    By Paul who made it resound;
But in the end he, too, was killed,
    His head rolled on the ground.

But in the years which followed this,
    Rome to Christ was turned;
No more were they to the lions given,
    Or as human torches burned.

Just think of people all so brave
    To give their lives for *Jesus;*
But don't you think *God* made it up,
    They're happier far to leave us.

For such was their influence then,
    That now the whole world through,
Christianity is the base of laws,
    And none are found more true.

So, as *Jesus* to us said,
    If we believe not in *Him;*
The work which *He* laid down for us,
    Will keep us all from sin.

The devil watches on every side,
    Some victim yet to know;
And once he gains us to his side,
    From *Christ* we're sure to go.

All the laws of every land
    Which makes this world the better
Are the nations and the lands
    Which follow *Him* to the letter.

* * *

PREPAREDNESS

"It seems you grow sweeter every day,"
    Said he to his wife,
Who looked with pride upon her Fred
    Who'd taken her for life.

Why, you might have married rich
    And been a social queen."
"Oh, don't say that," she softly replied,
    With a love so clearly seen.

"What would I do without you, now?"
    He quickly made reply.
"And what of me, did you ever think—
    Supposing you should die?"

"Well, little girl, I've thought of that
    Several times this year,
But I have saved you from all wants,
    I have this policy here."

"Now, Fred, you know I didn't intend
  To mean it just that way,
But now my heart would broken be
  Should you be taken away."

"There, there, my darling only one,
  Let us not think again
That anything can cross our sun,
  In this big world of men.

"In this big world of men," said she;
  "Do you know what I'm thinking?
No, Fred, of course you can not know."
  He felt his heart a-sinking.

He knew of what she was thinking now,
  Of church they'd never joined;
For he claimed the missions were
  Just people to catch your coin.

"You don't have to give to missions, Fred;
  Dear heart, it almost kills me—
You are as good as some in church,
  But, dear, that won't ever save thee."

"Ah, little girl, you've made a hit,
  I can't and won't dispute it;
But there's many sins your Fred must fight
  Before he can begin it."

"Oh, Fred, don't say that every time,
  It really brings me sorrow;
Don't you repent? Believe, don't you?
  Then confess *Him* before tomorrow."

"Ah, darling wife, I will," he said,
  As he bestowed his kiss;
"I've got to get to town tonight,
  Tomorrow I'll settle this."

"You've made me, oh, so happy dear!"
  And when she saw him leaving,
"Tomorrow night will show the world
  Both of us believing."

Tomorrow night—it never came—
  For just as she was sleeping,
They brought him home, so stark and cold,
  And joy was changed to weeping.

"An accident upon the car,"
  She heard somebody speaking;
But thank the Lord, he's just insured,
  A pauper he'll not be leaving."

And then a shriek, it smote the air;
  They heard his wife's voice ringing,
"Oh, *God!* He meant to do the right!"
  She started wildly singing.

Now God looks down and knows the heart—
  And had he not confessed?
Not to the world as *God* would have,
  He willed to do the rest.

But think of that heart-broken wife,
  Who hoped to meet him there.
Let us not judge the *King of Glory,*
  He'll treat him square, up. there .

Not very long after he had gone,
  His darling followed, too;
And let us hope they're happy now,
  Beyond those skies of blue.

But how much better had it been
  If earlier he'd confessed; .
There'd be no doubt in any mind
  Of their being now at rest.

JUST "KIDS"

You see, I'm just ten years old,
　But gee! I ain't a baby;
And once in a great big, big while
　Daddy calls me a little lady.

But most of people calls us "kids,"
　— And that I don't near like;
If mamma heard them call me that,
　You bet she'd make them hike.

It's "us kids, do this or that,"
　Or "kids, don't start to cry";
And all the fun we go to have,
　They stop us kids—now why?

Of course, a kid will holler some,
　But let me recolate,
If we don't do just this or that,
　It seems us kids they hate.

When Jenny had the tonsilitis,
　Right in her throat,
Her daddy said, "What is it, kid?"
　She asked him, "Who's de goat?"

Und say, it made him mad—
　He liked to never got through
A-whippin' Jenny after that—
　But don't you think 'twas true?

We like to run and have a time
　Out in the biggest barn,
Un' one day Tommy he felled down,
　Un' purt near broke his arm.

Now, Tommy is the sweetest kid,
    Un' one night at a party,
Un' jes cause he dropped me the handkerchief,
    The other kids called him smarty.

But say! When summer comes along,
    When on the farm it's fine,
We kids can sometime go out there—
    Und gee! We have a time!

Mamma whipped me one day
    Because I teased a pig;
I scared him underneath the fence,
    Und you orter seen him dig!

The hole, you know, wasn't big enough
    To let the pig right through;
Und that there pig was such a-a fool
    He didn't know what to do.

If he had backed two inches back
    His head would all been free,
But he kept a-pushin' und squealin' there;
    But a pig can't ever see.

When Tom pushed me in the horse trough,
    Uncle Jim jes laughed and hollered;
He said I looked 'bout like a pig
    Who'd been in a hog waller.

Und there wus a mans come to our house,
    His clothes wus old and dusty;
Und Tom, he punched me in the side
    Und said, "Don't he look rusty?"

He called at me und I went up,
    For Tom said I'd holler;
But he put his dirty arm around
    My nice und bestes' collar.

Und don't you know, that he bawled,
  Right there, you know, before us,
Because, he said, he'd had a home
  Und couldn't help but love us.

"Us," he said, and left off the "kid";
  Did I like him some, I wonder?
Fer Uncle Jim had allers said
  Kids was a nuisance, "by thunder."

But yer tramp I'm talkin uv,
  He said that kids was nice;
That if 'tweren't fer all us kids,
  Folks soon ud fergit 'bout Christ.

* * *

THE POWER OF ENVIRONMENT

It was the first morning of school,
  And the school house had one room;
But every boy and girl who came
  Looked to me for a boon.

As they came trooping in that morn
  They were a study indeed—
Here at hand was sure a chance
  To sow some golden seed.

How I remember one clean lad,
  About nine or ten, I guess;
His clothes were old, but very neat;
  His hair was combed and dressed.

He had a smile so sweet and dear,
  It lighted all around;
He was as square as square could be,
  I found, on the playground.

No use to tell how this boy did
    In all the examinations;
"Ah!" thought I to myself one day,
    "He may yet rule this nation."

I met his parents and you know,
    They were what I expected—
For such boys come from the homes
    Who are for truth respected.

They were so poor in this world's goods
    It really grieved my heart,
And made me pray for this same boy
    When to town they did depart.

I knew that father and mother, too,
    Would do their very best;
But Jack would have to have some friends,
    And could not change the rest.

If he had been, say eight years more,
    It might have been much better;
He was only ten when they moved, you know—
    For a while he'd write a letter.

But in a year or two from then,
    I lost him from my working;
I did not know who were his friends,
    Nor whether he was shirking.

I'd never, never thought the last,
    And thought that he would never
Bring sorrow on those parents dear,
    Who thought their Jack so clever.

Imagine my sorrow and surprise,
    As in the twilight glow,
I read of boys who bandits were,
    And Jack was there, you know!

How could it be our little Jack,
  Who surely now was twenty,
Could blow a safe, with covered face,
  When he surely had a plenty?

A plenty of the needed things,
  For his father hadn't failed,
Was working now to keep his boy—
  To find him now in jail.

I felt for those dear parents there,
  And went to hear their story;
They said that Jack forgot his work,
  To hurry after "glory."

Glory in deeds of daring boys,
  The mother to me wept,
"He saw the shooting in the shows,
  And from his feet was swept."

He wouldn't study any more,
  Every night meant a show,
Where he admired the Western Bill—
  Shooting men, you know.

These pictures had gone to his mind;
  And mother herself blaming,
For they had failed to go to church
  Every Sunday, she was claiming.

Dear old mother, once again,
  Took to herself the trouble,
When Jack's ways were not from her—
  He felt her talk was "bubbles."

It wasn't the father or mother dear—
  These parents weren't to blame—
But that "stuff" he got at the picture show
  Set his young mind aflame.

A mind that might have done great work
　　To help the world along,
A picture show had swallowed up,
　　And now he'd gone all wrong.

The pictures, yes, may be a good thing;
　　Education is their "tooting";
But not a simpering little queen
　　Saved by a gun man's shooting.

Let them really teach the world
　　Some glorifying lesson.
And then, instead of evil thoughts,
　　The young will get a blessing.

Some one says, why is it done—
　　Some crazed, some shooting, some funny?
Because the crowd demands that sort of thing,
　　Or the "box" will receive no money.

So it's the call of the main crowd
　　For gun and cattle ranging;
If we refuse to see such "stuff,"
　　The pictures shall soon be changing.

They all reflect the public mind,
　　The thing for which they're longing,
And so the crowd who yells for them
　　Show where they are belonging.

Now, there are pictures good to see,
　　Of daring, yet good behavior;
Of brave men fighting for the right,
　　Without guns—for their *Saviour*.

WHO'S TO BLAME?

In a hall where all was splendor,
  As amid the dancing throng
Whirled a pretty little maiden,
  From whose heart there came a song.

Her pretty hair and velvet shoulders
  Gleamed in lights of whitest hue;
"I don't believe in churches, Charley;
  Really now, my dear, do you?

"I'm as good as Mrs. Thornton
  Who gives card parties every night,
And gambles for some pretty present,
  Bad as any bad man—am I right?"

In the morning, bright and golden,
  Sits a man who's well content;
He gives much to all the missions,
  But kicks out all who pay no rent."

"I'm as good as he, I know it,"
  Said a gambler who saw the sight;
"No use of joining any churches,
  When I'm doing more than he that's right."

In an alley, cold and freezing,
  Walks a tramp who's well nigh dead;
Then he thinks of love and home folks,
  And 'twould surprise you what he said:

"I used to think that all the Christians,
  Or the ones who went to prayer,
Were no better than the balance—
  If they reach Heaven, I'll be there."

So, dear people, here is shown
    The kinds of people we know and see—
So take Christ's warning while we're here,
    For Christ has shown the way for thee.

"I'm as good as a church member,"
    Say so many, proud and gay;
But we can but take the Bible,
    If we ever find the way.

To where all is joyful living,
    Where every heart is good and true;
A church member may be wanting,
    But *Heaven* itself is up to you.

STONES MAY FLY

Stones may fly, and I wonder why,
    Among the Christians here;
Saul began the Christians to end,
    Back in the bygone years.

But what caused all the throws
    Aimed at Stephen then?
As Saul stood by and held the clothes
    Until there came the end.

Suffering along God's way,
    Stephen sought to go;
But Saul found out what 'twas about
    And would not have it so.

Did Saul think that he was right?
    Of course he did, 'twas said;
But *that* and God did not ease much
    The sainted Stephen's end.

But now, let's see what was the end
    Of all these throws at him:
Saul started down to Damascus town,
    Against Christ he worked with vim.

Saul took many men along
    To bring Christ's followers in;
When from the sky came such a light,
    He fell—it blinded him.

"Who art Thou, Lord?" Saul did say;
    A voice came from on high:
"Saul, Saul, why persecutest thou Me?"
    Others heard that voice near by.

We all know how Saul was turned
    From the speaker blind,
But to Christ his efforts were given,
    Forever from this time.

His name was changed unto Paul,
    And even to Rome, he went;
Now, perhaps this was God's plan,
    For His work to there be sent.

So you, too, may receive a stone,
    God has his own ends;
Poor Stephen was stoned to earth,
    But it saved many men.

When little stones at you fly,
    Like those of tongue or pen,
Remember this, it may be God;
    He'll always make amends.

There's nothing here that's quite so dear
    As when you come to die,
That you have striven for the world,
    Although the stones do fly.

"GUILTY, YOUR HONOR, GUILTY"

"Trouble and grief o'er the loss of my child,"
    Seemed to a mother, 'twould drive her wild;
But don't be forgetting that on the way
    A hand will be helping; I hear Him say:
"Come unto me all weary and worn,
    Unto a new life your girl has been born."

As she lay sleeping, an angel she seemed,
    As over the casket the warm sun beamed;
She's always been faithful, and now you will know
    It never had been better to have her to go;
And though we say it, it's hard to believe,
    While those who have loved her can never but grieve.

But come with me in your imagination,
    See one just as sweet brought to the station,
Though your dear one, never likely to meet,
    Would have kept hold and always been sweet;
Yet, never forget that this life is long,
    There's always a chance for one to go wrong.

We'll gather this morning along with the rest,
    And see what the police court offers, at best:
They brought in a maiden, not much like the rest,
    For she was so pretty, and dressed in the best—
Of black—it seemed mourning—and from her eye—
    "Some one is dead?" No, that isn't why.

Her charge, they say, 'twas walking out late,
    And it seemed 'twas enough to seal her fate;
"If that's the charge, Judge, I'm guilty, you know—
    But why I am guilty I'd like to say so."
The judge, he assented with a nod of his head.
    "I wasn't out walking," 'twas all she said.

"You may look and upbraid me as one with a crime,
    A deep-dyed character has never been mine;
I once loved a man as poor as could be,

And "Obey your own mother," he once said to me;
My mother, she her own words were lent,
  And forced the young man from me to be sent.

"My child, he is no companion for thee;
  "He lacketh the money," she then said to me.
Then I met Charley, that proud young man,
  Who wooed and won me—won my hand.
The time for the wedding was set for a year;
  The happiness of it to me was most dear.

When for the wedding the final day came,
  He left me to mourn him, and mourn him in shame—
To die, thus to hide my folly and shame,
  For never could baby hold his own name.
He claimed to be noble, be generous, and true,
  And made me beieve it to the last moment, too.

When baby came, he lived but an hour;
  Could he have lived 'twould have given me power,
And now I must go over there with the rest;
  If baby were here, his wrongs I'd redress.
If Charley should go to that same filthy jail
  It would soon be forgotten by some pretty female.

But you who so scorn me now to behold,
  Will try to make him a man with a soul;
You will forget anything I have said,
  And snatch up Charley, just to be wed
To riches, for his one little fling—
  That's what you call it—my own soul's sting.

While men can forget and others do, too,
  What in the world can a poor girl do?
All of my sorrow I'll never live down,
  For your Honor will order for me to leave town—
His plaything forgotten, again will he live,
  And at his mansion, his banquets will give.

While I, all degraded, will have to leave town—
    Ruined—yes ruined—for you'll help it resound;
But God up above loves women as well
    As any proud fellow who lures her to hell;
And for a fellow like Charley, you know,
    There'll be little rest—God won't have it so.

And those who have unwisely followed love's behest,
    When repenting and saddened, with *God'll* find rest.''
Here she stopped speaking, her head sadly bent,
    When forth stepped a lady who hadn't been sent;
She wasn't supposed to be in the play,
    But she did *Christ's* part for the girl, anyway.

''Poor girl, your mother is lost unto you?''
    A nod of the head showed it to be true.
''Poor girl, I'm sorry you've been fooled by a cad,
    But dear heart, remember the men aren't all bad.
No, I'll be your mother a long way from here,
    You'll still have a home and all that's dear.

''This awful memory, I believe you will see,
    'Twill help you be better than ever you'd be.
What's the fine, Judge?'' ''Not a cent,'' he replied,
    And along with the rest, a tear strove to hide.
''Well, you've got a heart for not taking a cent.''
    So they turned to the door, and away they both went.

Now, God looks down upon us below,
    And when the day comes He'll know what is so;
And remember the words before He went home,
    ''Let him without sin cast the first stone.''

HOW DO WE KNOW?

How much a little love may do
　　To help in life's great storm,
When things are bad and very sad
　　And you wonder why you've been born.

Just why you to earth were sent,
　　When no good you can do;
But there are those with great deeds
　　Who work with just the few.

Dark and dreary, life may seem,
　　When there comes a little ray,
A ray of light, as from the home
　　You had in bygone days.

Oh, those who may have their health,
　　You never stop to think
How far from the crowd's sight
　　An invalid wants to shrink.

For it gets old, so very old,
　　To hear them come this way;
"How is our friend here today?"
　　"About the same," they say.

About the same, about the same,
　　From one day to another;
But it may do your own heart good
　　If you have helped a brother.

Because if, in this pain of life,
　　You patiently keep up here,
It will decide some other life,
　　They'll face it with less fear.

Of all sad words of tongue or pen,
　　Are the words "It might have been";
But when you're down you might yet try
　　To get right up again.

For some come and some go,
　　And then get, oh, so tired,
That you wish you'd been in France
　　When first the Germans fired.

It doesn't do to sit and cry
　　When sorrows surely come;
The best thing to say, if dead,
　　"I'll then go home."

Yes, go home where all is rest
　　From our mortal pain,
Where we can run and get tired
　　And then rest again.

Now, some feel that Heaven must
　　Be a place of rest;
Health to run and play and work
　　Would be Heaven's best.

Now, the ones who have their health,
　　But must toil their best,
Could in Heaven have such fun
　　If they could but rest.

So I guess it's even up;
　　We'll all get what we need,
If we ever even up
　　And kill the devil's seed.

For the devil sows his seed
　　In every home and place,
And if we ever beat him here,
　　We've got to run the race.

We can't stand back and talk of it,
　　Saying it's all no go,
For then you're helping to stifle love,
　　And the devil his seed to sow.

THE CEREMONY

Two fathers sat in their chairs,
Two mothers gave what was theirs;
The bride, in such beauty born,
Seemed like the rays of the rising morn.

Why is a father's face so grave?
Why weeps a mother for the daughter gave?
Why weeps a mother for a son so brave?
Is this a wedding, or is it the grave?
Now, the thing that here causes tears—
'Tis not for the daughter one fears,
'Tis not for the son, another has;
But 'tis the doubt that always wears
The parents hearts; they only care,
Thinking of wrongs their child must bear;
Now, this need never have been so
If both had told the truth, you know.

And the first picture which we give
Is the one all men should live;
It is the one all girls should tell—
It decides whether home is home or hell.

But why can't they take another air?
Why can't they see how each one cares?
Why can't they see her look divine,
As upon her face is the look, "He's mine,
Mine, for the coming years,
When love shall wash away all tears"?
For he has told her all the fears
That she may know in future years,
The load they both must take;
He's told her all for her own sake.
What sort of home she's going to,
And now, she feels it will be true.
Why must tears be started then,
Even by the best of men?
If both love each other here,
That home is God's nest so dear.

But suppose there is a *lie*,
Suppose he has told her why
He can support her in great style,
And been a-lying all the while;
When he can never, never do—
The things he says will never come true.
Look at that sweet, trusting bride,
Who has opened her arms so wide,
To receive a trusted, worthy man!
Oh! Life will end where it began.
Suppose, you know, it's not his sin
That in the home the trouble begins;
Suppose he's told her how he's poor,
The wolf may sometimes be at their door—
Yet, to him, she seems not to care;
She'll follow him just anywhere.
Then, when the home life they begin,
She rails of *poor* being his sin.
Suppose the wolf comes to the door:
"Oh! This is hell; I'll stay no more!"
And then she drops from her place,
Leaving him the world to face.

Now, these are what the parents think
As they see their offspring on the brink
Of taking up another life,
Choosing a husband and a wife;
They know that there are many shoals
Which bring down so many souls,
And that is why they shed a tear—
'Tis for a daughter or a son so dear.

But listen again before I cease,
Let your mind these things release:
Homes are our country's very hope,
And God's, too; why sit and mope?
This is a couple dear—
For them, let's leave out the fear,
For each has told all there is to know,

And each can stand the trouble; so
'Tis a blessing for each, and there
All were young once; can't you bear
To see the loving ones out there?
The old world's trouble, they will share.
Pray that each may have long life,
And conquer in their own strife;
For maybe you feel no good's the man
Who's taken your own daughter's hand,
But he may be more than true,
For if she died with "God bless you,"
Would you think she had happy been,
Or the man had wrought a deadly sin?

Don't expect this new daughter to know
Just how to darn each heel and toe;
Don't expect her, yet, to bake
The nicest and the sweetest cake;
For if each family that's behind
Will return, in their own mind,
In the days when they were young,
They may remember words that stung,
Stung just like the words these hear;
But you didn't care, you didn't care.
For God knows how the wanderer roams,
And always a-thinking of a home, sweet home;
For home is home where *she* may be,
No mansion makes *his* home, you see.
Now, if in them you something dislike,
It's better than divorce, to keep it quiet.
Life, along with its breakers and foam,
May come to them, just—"Home Sweet Home."

JUST A DREAM

"You little, tear-stained, blue-eyed girl,
    What makes you weep so?
Oh! I see, you want the doll
    Which bats its eyes, you know.

"Well, here it is." Her eyes light up
    But for a moment, when
She drops her doll on the floor—
    Its eyes won't work again.

Oh, how she cries! Her heart is broken,
    For never will she get
Another great big, big doll,
    Though she must fuss and fret.

"Now, as you go on through life,
    You'll find that all the things
Which seem so beautiful, a little way off,
    When secured, no pleasure brings.

"Did I say, no pleasure brings?
    "Well, I am wrong just here,
For life holds out such great, great things,
    You can't get all that's dear.

"One thing else you should sure get,
    And all the rest don't matter,
And that is 'love,' the greatest thing—
    Here, don't your toys all scatter."

She looked at me with saucy eyes,
    As though she didn't care;
Her mamma and her daddy, too,
    She seems to no wise fear.

"Come here, baby," said I then,
  "Now, give your daddy a hug,
And then I'll put you in your bed,
  As 'snug as a bug in a rug'."

"And mamma, too?" she then asked me,
  When her toes wriggled at the fire;
"Yes, and mamma will go to bed
  With her little child."

When from the office I returned,
  On this very night,
I sighed to think 'twas all a dream
  I'd had of baby bright.

And mamma, too—no such a one
  Blessed my noon-time years;
Perhaps they are better off,
  As I look up, through tears.

The baby, it is true enough,
  Though from my life it went;
And mamma, too, had left me here
  When a message from God was sent.

It matters not what people may seem,
  What they seem in general;
But the death of a dream, sometimes, I know,
  Is to the one, like a funeral.

To stop amid God's dearest flowers,
  Or such they surely seem,
Is like death, when you see the flower
  Is growing, oh God, from Thee.

WHICH WAY?

As I sat in the warm sunshine,
    On that beautiful morning in May,
My tired nerves relaxed,
    My mind was given its way.

I guess if the truth were known,
    I slept and nodded there,
While about me hummed the bees,
    As I slept there in my chair.

But a wonderful change, it came to me,
    For I stood on a high plateau;
The top must have been wonderful to see,
    Though my back was turned to it all.

Yes, I sat on the edge of a cliff,
    Looking down the steep incline;
I knew that the light behind
    Was brighter than any sunshine.

For the sweetest sounds I e'er heard
    Came floating from behind;
'Twas music of the sainted souls,
    Once belonging to the world's mankind.

I would have turned to look at them,
    But the sight I saw far below
Caused me the chimes to forget
    As I sat gazing down there, you know.

"I wonder what all of that means?"
    I thought in my wondering way;
"It is life, and you see the strife;
    Should you wish a while longer to stay?"

The voice, as from an angel,
    Floated into my ears;
I wanted to see what life held,
    But I had my qualms and fears.

For I knew I had suddenly gone
    From my porch and humming bees;
I wondered if I had died,
    And my family no longer would see.

But, it seemed, that up that slope
    Some had arrived like me,
But I didn't feel tired, you know,
    And looked for all I could see.

Down, down, at the bottom there,
    There was a striving band;
All kinds of people, you know, were there—
    People from every land.

Some were shouting out commands,
    As from a little guide book;
He pointed to a dismal way,
    All slush and a muddy brook.

Another held the same guide book
    And roared as loud as any;
He pointed to no way at all,
    Though around him were many.

It seemed as if to him was given
    The same little book;
"But you don't know how to read,"
    And he wouldn't give them a look.

"Pray to me, and I'll take you up,"
    It seemed I heard his cry;
This satisfied more men
    Than the others who made reply.

Another held on to his book,
    But never opened it;
"It's all in the way you think you know,
    You'll go if you are fit."

There was a river they had to cross,
    Where Christ had been one day;
Though He was immersed by John the Baptist,
    For the book told of that way.

There came a band to this same stream,
    They stood just for a second, .
And then they built a bridge o'er it,
    "That's just as good, we reckon."

Another crowd who had the book
    Also came along—
"Behold Baptism, jump in deep,
    Then you can do no wrong."

Others came with a leader tall,
    He stopped and took a look;
"But you must stop six months before
    "You jump into this brook."

But at last I saw a band,
    The Book they always read;
They came unto the River Jordan,
    And like Jesus they were led.

Led into its waters there,
    The Book held by the man,
Said, "This doth not end the race,
    Go on to the better land."

And then they, pausing not to tarry,
    They took up their weary way;
For it was a weary, trying time,
    As the crowds hooted alway.

I now found out for the first time,
　The hill was only life;
And there were spots so beautiful
　That some kept from the strife.

"We're just as good as they,
　And we have got the money;
No use to follow a fool guide book,
　It really seems so funny."

While others sat down in the brush,
　Though burrs and nettles pricked;
"Oh, I am tired to hear them talk,
　It only makes me sick."

The last two kinds seemed well content,
　Though they knew of the place
Where I sat and gazed at them,
　But I never saw their face.

Excepting once, a fellow turned
　And gazed up at me,
Falling down upon the ground,
　He no farther got, you see.

Poor fellow, he no farther got,
　For he had forgotten God;
To keep the world as pure as possible,
　They laid him under the sod.

But all at once a pain came
　Into my neck so sharp,
For a little bug had had a nip,
　And the place did truly smart.

I started up and almost fell
　From my chair, it seems;
For all of the thing which I saw
　Must have been a dream.

FORGOTTEN HEROES

Did you ever, in a shipyard,
  See the wrecks brought from the sea?
Never more to cast an anchor
  Or make sail for some new lee.
If these ships could tell their story,
  They most interesting would sound;
But remember as you view them
  The human wrecks about a town.
Perhaps you find them in police court,
  Giving forth a plea of woe,
While the judge sits perhaps attentive,
  And you wonder if 'tis so;
Is it true, the story told us
  Of the poor old gray-haired man—
How he once was young and happy;
  Loved as much as any can;
To do right and much be honored;
  Stand a bulwark to his home;
Now a wreck, just after sailing
  Over life, nor found his own
Place in life where he was happy?
  Though so humbly he upward looks
At the judge to catch some pity,
  As he glances through his books.
He was old and very ragged,
  Tottered when he tried to walk.
Why was this poor lonely beggar
  Brought to court and made to talk?
Seems the judge had grown impatient
  While the man made no reply,
So again he sharply asked him,
  "That's your sentence; answer why,
If there be a real good reason,
  Why this court should not consent
That to prison you be abandoned,
  Why to jail you be not sent."
Then this worn and wasted figure
  Seemed some taller yet to grow,

And he raised his gaunt old person
　　And said he'd guess he'd have to go.
"Yes, your honor, I am guilty
　　Of the charge that ye have sent,
But to do a mortal evil
　　Never had been my intent.
Once I was young and not bad-looking,"
　　This he said with a sad smile,
As he looked upon the crowd
　　As they listened all the while,
But a thought which next came to him
　　Brought a tear from eyes well spent,
For he'd often been a-crying
　　'Cause he hadn't paid the rent.
Rent, he knew, must be forthcoming,
　　Or they'd turn him to the street;
So he gathered up some plunder
　　So the rent he might yet meet;
Then he told them how he'd sold it
　　To a junk dealer who came that way:
A little baby's worn-out clothing,
　　And his wife's, his bill to pay.
"Sure, I've had those things a good time,
　　And to me they seemed most dear,
And you see that in the parting
　　I couldn't help but shed a tear.
And I did a guilty doing
　　Just to get those dear duds back,
And was just a-sneakin' with 'em
　　When the cop gave me this whack."
Then he pulled his hair to one side
　　And a bloody place we saw,
And to those as has some feelings,
　　Toward our justice we felt raw;
But he was guilty of law-breaking,
　　And the law must take its course,
But when his honor pronounced the sentence
　　His own voice was somewhat hoarse.
"Would you please to kindly tell us
　　Why some work you have not found?
Is that cripple just a make-shift?

Do you do it to fool the town?"
Then he answered to his honor,
    "I have never been so low;
I was caught right through the knee, sir,
    Shootin' rebs at old Shiloh;
But the best friend that I ever
    Had, who did me a good turn,
Was a southern true-born gentleman—
    Now I've said it, though I burn!
Take and put me in your prison,
    I have suffered at Andersonville;
And I 'low that all your sufferin'
    'Tain't as that, if ye want to kill."
"Stop!" was heard near the doorway.
    "What's the sum of that man's fine?"
"Just ten dollars," said his honor,
    "Or take his choice and do the time."
"Why have you not gone, old soldier,
    To the home that's open to you?"
Said the young man who wore a suit
    Olive drab, and not of blue.
"Well my friend," the old man answered,
    "Home is home where'er it be,
And I have hung to a few reminders
    Which makes it now to jail with me."
"Never!" said the O. D. stranger,
    "I have been in hell as well as you,
I've fought the Germans near the Rhineland,
    I wore the O. D. and you the blue;
But let me say to you, old comrade,
    I've lost a wife since I went "over there";
And come and stop with me, old comrade,
    And have some days more bright and fair."
Now this, it seemed to please the old man,
    Who left the room almost with joy,
And now he's telling how his comrades
    Were made of men like this same boy.
And so you see, justice found its wishes—
    A heart made glad by this young man's trod,
And don't you reckon we'll all be comrades
    When it comes to lying beneath the sod?

A STAR

Supposing the sun should rise for you,
   And when it stood o'erhead,
Turn back to the east and set again,
   Would it not cause much dread?

Dread, that all was over for you,
   That stars would surely cease,
That for this life your work was done,
   That for life you'd lost your lease.   ,

Has it ever happened unto you,
   This dreadful thing, I say?
Or has your sun made its regular run,
   And happiness been your way?

Now this, unless you see with me,
   Is all a warped delusion;
You say my mind is crazed, you know;
   That would be your conclusion.

But did you ever meet a star,
   A soul in a beautiful form,
Though, like the sun was rising up,
   Some soul in beauty born?

They started, like the sun, their earthly course,
   And gave brightness unto all—
Brightness of smiles and good deeds done—
   And then began to fall.

At first, 'twas but a weariness;
   They felt so tired and blue,
But kept on smiling all day long,
   As was their wont to do.

It's not long, life gives us our chance
 To bring our talents to light;
We make the plans for God, unless
 We're afraid to make the fight.

But a strange pallor covers her face,
 And a flush is on her cheek;
No one, it seems, can think it true,
 But she feels the fall of feet.

Feet that's making a forward march,
 There's a pain in her chest;
Tuberculosis had done its deed
 Before she's told the rest.

It is the noon-time of her life,
 A happy woman is she;
She's saved more souls by generous words
 Than many who are paid a fee.

But *God* has called her back to *Him,*
 Where she's in Heaven's band;
We know not why this thing must be,
 "But some time we'll understand."

Why can't we all follow her work—
 . We who are so strong?
Why, if we'd follow out her plan,
 The sinners might soon be gone.

We saw her only for a while,
 But she's not gone so far;
And up in Heaven, just like her,
 We, too, may win a star.

AS GOOD AS THEY

It was a beautiful morning in May;
    Even the grass and flowers
Seemed in accord with the sunshine
    To make beautiful hours.

Hours of memories long gone by,
    Which could but be happy now,
For the balmy freshness of that hour
    Was as the fragrance of flowers.

It was a wonderful morning of Sunday,
    And the day seemed blessed;
We met a man of sober mein,
    Going to churh, well dressed.

Strangers were we in this city,
    But to my pal and me
The reverend stranger never bowed nor spoke.
    "He feels he's too good, you see.

"Such are all the churches,"
    Spoke my friend at my side,
For he believed that churches all were bad;
    He had only seen from outside.

"Let's go out and hunt up a meeting or a church,"
    I said that evening, with fear,
For just to be plain, I wanted this friend;
    No one else near was dear.

But Charley was not so narrow in mind
    As to bar one, there and then;
He was an actor and studied characters,
    He watched the style of men.

I knew he held no interest in going
    Except the people to see;
But when we left we started to talk,
    For he was kind to me.

He knew I had felt a good inspiration
    In being there at all;
"But don't you think the ones out of church
    Are no more liable to fall?"

He started then some example to give—
    The ones who said they were good—
And gave to me examples strong,
    And here is how it stood.

"The dance sped on," he did the speaking,
    "Midst lights of whitest hue,
And as her lover clasped her waist,
    Was he a lover, true?

"They both belonged to a swell church,
    Believed in dancing halls;
But you can't make me think it right—
    Christ-like. Not at all.

"The rich man sat at home in ease,
    He, much to missions sent;
But kicked the poor man from his house
    If he failed to pay his rent.

"I'm just as good as he dare be,"
    A gambler said who knew;
"I gamble some to pay my way,
    But he's a gambler, too.

If to Heaven he ever goes
    And gets to stay and see,
I'm not worrying on my part,
    I'm just as good as he."

"In an alley dark and cold,
    A tramp was well nigh spent,
But church was going on that night
    And toward the light he went.

"They found him dead, there in the snow,
    The very next morning;
Now, some had seen him the night before,
    But did not give warning."

How could I answer for the church?
    How could I set him right?
I hardly knew just what to say
    To make *Christ's* suffering right.

"Dear friend," I said to him right then,
    "This case sure looks bad,
But let me tell you some things;
    I'll convince you or be so sad.

"*Christ* tells all that we must do
    To get to Heaven and win:
Believe, confess and *be baptized*
    For the remission of sin."

"They've all done that, you know," he said;
    He felt he sure had me.
"*Jesus* died for all our souls, you know;
    He's waiting now to save thee.

"After the baptizing's done, dear friend,
    We've got to *Christians* be;
And when you tell *God* they were the cause,
    He'll have nothing, then, for thee.

It won't save your soul at all, old boy,
    You got to do your part;
Not just on Sunday must it come,
    But from your very heart."

THE FRIEND'S DEATH

Did you ever experience a funeral
    Without a corpse or shroud,
At least not earthly noticed here,
    Nor proclaimed by a weeping crowd?

Did you ever to your life's own heart
    A friend in great faith take—
One you love well enough
    To die for his own sake?

Did you take and honor him,
    And tell him all your life
That on equal terms you still might be,
    And help shield each from strife?

Then, when there was so much faith,
    You'd stand, you felt, for him—
Only to find his vows all false,
    When your heart felt so grim?

This has happened, perhaps to you,
    You've had a friend, you thought,
When all at once you found right out
    'Twas only favors sought.

And yet, more tragic has it seemed
    When you thought he worked for Christ,
That he could talk and work with vim,
    But was weak in paying the price.

His old world habits, he'd kept on,
    And several other sins,
Which were kept hidden from every eye
    When at first he begins.

But let the truth carry on,
    Though this friend be dead;
Perhaps he'll do a great work,
    Though shackled as with lead.

You can not deny the work,
    Though the heart of him be gone;
These secret sins, like fungus growth,
    Will pierce the living one.

Our own sins, you know, will find us out,
    Sooner than later here;
But for a friendship to die and rot—
    'Tis as a death were near.

* * *

A FRIENDLY GAME

"Come on, old man, let's go to town,
And let the girls have their round;
Let's go down to the club,"
Then in a whisper, "Have a rub."
"Now, you two boys just want to get
Away from home, that's all, I bet."
And Sally came up to John,
While Margaret said, "Jim, stay on;
You're more than all the world, you bet,
Another Jim I can never get."
"I won't be gone long, my pet;
When we come home, you'll be up yet."

These two couples were very young,
And in each heart a song was sung;
They'd been acquainted many years,
God's holy love had brought no tears.
The girls insisted that Jim and John
Would be good boys and yet stay on!
For this is the first night, you know,
That John and Sally have come here so."

"Jim, you won't be mean tonight,
When it's just one year ago." "That's right,"
Jim made his own, his best reply.
Yet John, the girls seemed to defy.
"Ah, come on," at last John said;
"If this keeps up, I'll wish I were dead."
Away they went with both content;
They knew how evenings they had spent.
Oh! Their wives might fuss a bit,
But both would soon get over it.

So John was saying as he went along;
They both were men so stout and strong.
"Say, does your wife know we play cards?"
Jim asked, as they sat in the car.
"Sally? Jim, you understand
A fellow can't join an angel band
Because he's married the nicest girl
That's to be found in all the world.

"Well," said Jim, "I have my fears;
Margaret is the best of girls;
I wouldn't hurt her feelings for worlds,
And I hate those tears which come to her eyes
When of the cards I tell her lies.
Lies are not the bestest thing
To use with her; it leaves a sting.
And when my Margaret sings a song
It seems to me I've many a wrong."

"Ah! Cut that stuff, Jim old pal,
We can't do all to please the 'gals';
But thank the Lord," John replied,
Sally was brought up outside
This card-revolting screen;
And many times I have seen
Her mother's parties, behind a shade,
Playing bridge for a bauble for which dad had paid."

"Yes, I know your people don't care,
You feel it just and only fair;
But we get excited when
We've got a pretty big pot and then
We say some things we sometimes hate;
Sometimes, you know, I think too late.
Now, I don't know the game like you;
Perhaps if I did, I could better keep cool;
But as it is I am a great fool
About all our little social games."

"Oh come, let's get out of this,
You'll spoil the fun, we must not miss,
For when are you going to do
The buying of the car, so new?"

"Well, I haven't decided yet."

"Now Jim, you make the greatest hit
With all the ladies that are it;
And when a car you go to buy
You must remember Sally and I,
For if you don't hurry fast
To get that car, you may be last;
But then, if I get a car before,
I expect it would be at your door
About as much as it is at mine,
So whoever gets it, we'll both say fine."

"That's the talk I like to hear,
For John, you've always been so dear,
For even Margaret, who is mine,
Might ride in your own limousine."

Jim did not care to leave the girls,
To go out taking these midnight whirls.
They talked along in this vein
Until they both left their train
And were in their chairs upstairs.

When they both had taken a seat,
The waiter came around to meet;
And asked them what he could do
To make the evening go right through.
Jim sat in silence all the while,
A-thinking yet of Margaret's smile,
When he in playful mood had said,
"I'll work for her until I'm dead,
Or have a handsome limousine
And show the folks right down the line."
He's thinking now of what John has said,
And of the gambling of which he'd read.
He thought how people in their homes
Proclaimed that cards kept boys at home;
He remembered his old mother fair,
With silky locks of pearl-gray hair;
Remembered as from the country home,
He'd left his pa and ma to roam;
How, when he'd taken Margaret there,
They had told her how their Jim was square,
They'd trust him with the lives of theirs;
Had never caused them any cares;
How he was honest, good and true,
And now he thinks they told her, too,
That the point wherein his weakness lay,
Was letting companions take him away
      When he least expected.
And that they felt, oh, so glad
Some foolish girl hadn't made him mad;
For at the first they were enraptured
To think that such as her he'd captured.
Ah, better, better for him to be
With Margaret out in the sunshine free!

His mind was made up to the letter
To buy a limousine or better,
But yet he only has half enough.
Had John just said things as a bluff?
Suppose this night right here,
Over their cards and some beer,

John should win all he had
Saved for a machine, good or bad.
He wouldn't be such a cad
As not to live up to the letter;
So to John he makes the offer,
"We'll play the game to bottoms coffer;
Then if I should all of it lose,
You the auto then will choose;
And if, old man, I should happen to win,
I'd consider it a deadly sin
      If I treated you no better."

"Of course I'll do that, you know.
Here! Give us a new deck; give it a throw.
Because I'm going to give you a race,
For buying a machine, I feel, is my place."
And as John caught the waiter's eye,
A glance was passed Jim on the sly,
Which caused the man to change a pack,
And fix it up at John's own back;
But a mirror stood before the table,
And John was an old fish for card labels.
He could read a back as well as a face—
He knew what Jim always had in place.
Now, they had stayed until two a. m;
These fellows were excited, and were no more men.
John got the tip he had given the boy—
An extra ace, the deck now bore.
At last, when there upon the table
Lay Jim's cash, and that's no fable;
'Twas all he had; 'twas his all—
My God, he must win this or fall!
Why was John always raising a jump,
When he felt that he had the only trump;
He held a straight flush, he knew;
John couldn't have aces—they were too few.
At last Jim's nerves became a tingle,
He reached for his pocket and his fingers mingled
Among some old papers, all that he had,

And he felt something else that made him mad—
    His own revolver!
He thought that he had left it at home,
But there it was to defend that home.
John noticed the excited face,
But felt he was thinking of Margaret's place
    In that limousine.
John didn't intend for it to go too far;
Jim now wished he'd never been there.
Both of them think of their wives in despair,   ·
Because it was three and they weren't there.
But John, you've failed in your jest—
You're playing in fun which never is blest.
Jim thinks it's all of it true,
He is angry that John sits so cool.

All, my God, with Margaret in tears;
Again under the table that John doesn't fear—
    Jim never carried a gun.

"I've covered it now, show up quick,
If you've duped me by some damnable trick,
    I'll have your blood!"

John, in surprise, threw down his cards,
And from the table started to rise.
"Yes, I knew that it surely must be,
Do you ever suppose I'll let you go free?"
Oh, why can't some see that gun quick?
John only meant a kindly trick,
But now he grows ashen and pale,
He fails to hear a warning hail.
Oh! Where are Sally and Margaret then?
Both left that evening by loving men—
One just a trick of cards has made,
The other to ashes imagines his home is laid.
With muscles distorted, his breath so hot,
The men all hear the deadly shot,
    And rush upstairs.

Poor Sally and Margaret, your hearts are not stone,
Made by the hell of a gambler's throne.
Some one says it's a terrible mistake—
They were both friends. Jim made an escape—
    Does that help those women?

John thought he could handle Jim;
Jim thought John was dishonoring him.
Under the sod now John's body lays,
And a dying wife receives a letter one day;
It came from the West—she should know
Jim died fighting for God's people below.
But both lives are blasted, and it's hard to say,
Can either forget their own past days?
Maybe they can and a reward will receive,
By some one who in dynamite does not believe.
For now the harm in cards, Sally can see—
The vice is the misunderstandings, believe me,
Whether playing for money or just after tea.
Little boys' eyes are bright here to see.
Don't live so any one can point, and be true,
Saying cards was their downfall—
    And that it was you.

*   *   *

OVER THERE

Over there, over there, do they care
    That we stand guard tonight,
Guard to those sleeping comrades there
    Who have come "over there" to fight?

Yes, some one cares; he's over there,
    That chap with light brown hair;
But here's another who thinks of mother,
    And she cares, he's "over there."

Today's hard battle, with its long rattle,
    Has been an awful slaughter;
And in the strife, one gave his life,
    The sweetheart of a daughter.

Tonight he sleeps beneath that heap
    Of soil that's "over there";
His God has come to guide him home,
    He'll never come from there.

Apart from there there sits old Joe,
    Though he had a right to sleep;
He watches the guard who's had it hard,
    And for the boy could weep.

For this boy's over there, over there,
    And a darling awaits at home,
And the picket men are in danger then,
    And the guard is thinking of home.

Joe sees in the brush a man creep slowly,
    And he fears for the others then;
Joe does not care that he is there,
    For he came with the very first men.

He does not care, he does not care,
    He's glad to be "over there";
He quickly fires where the guard sees not,
    And saves the guard over there.

Over there, over there, does any care
    That Joe came over there?
It saved the men who were there then,
    But Joe stays over there.

Over there, over there, some will care,
    For his soul went up that morn,
To where his soul will find a home,
    Though his face is bloody and torn.

Over there, over there, no one cares,
    They may have forgotten Joe;
But over there where there's no care,
    He'll find his Heaven, we know.

Over there, over there, do we all care?
    There's many who have returned,
But it's hard to remember the bodies rendered
    For our freedom over there.

"Over there, over there, we whipped the Dutch!"
    But who did the licking?
'Twas the boys who went from joys,
    To die for us, over there.

Don't forget their worthiness yet,
    As about they go disabled;
For perhaps like Joe, they'd rather go
    And lie in peace "over there."

Over there, over there, he doesn't care,
    He's glad, I expect, he's there;
For he went alone, he had no home,
    Just to fight for freedom there.

A GUIDING HAND

How can I deny a God
  When I have known you,
With eyes so blue 'neath beautiful hair,
  Who led me ever true?

Tonight it seems that you were born
  Only to love my soul;
And those last words, "God bless you, dear!"
  Make memories worth more than gold.

Amid my sickness and distress,
  With baby never near,
There's only one great blessing, dear,
  That holds me up, I fear.

And that is, dear father and mother,
  Who do for me each day;
But God alone I'm looking to
  To hold me on my way.

I love to feel that over there,
  You and I may meet;
And once again, about God's throne,
  Live without care, so sweet.

I've always been trying, but am not denying
  I often make a mistake,
But my mission here is to try to cheer
  Some one every day.

I try not to miss some great chance
  To do a noble deed,
But I'm awful blue at times, 'tis true,
  In the sowing of my seed.

For some may fall among the thorns,
    And be choked there;
And some on rocks may die of want,
    Be no good anywhere.

Brothers all, we may fall,
    But don't give up the strife;
Jesus died for our sins,
    Let's pray to *Him* for life.

For life to help a weary one,
    And always wear a smile;
Then we may hope we're with the *Son,*
    Find blessings in after life.

* * *

LIFE

Of all the songs which men have sung,
    And yet they find no boon;
They must commune with greater things
    Or we'll get out of tune.

Life goes on with sorrow or song,
    No matter what we do;
'Tis hard to gather all the threads
    Which lead to all that's true.

One loves the music of the bird,
    As on the twig he sings;
While some may travel and never gather
    This beauty as it rings.

Some follow up the higher plane,
    And pluck the roses there;
While others play the cities' game,
    But find no nature there.

A higher plane of thought and love,
    For God's in every line
Of the thing which we all call
    Nature. It is Divine.

Go forth at night and look above
    At the countless little stars;
"Who made these things?" you ask yourself—
    Does thus your ignorance bar?

How can you ever believe it, then?
    As at the stars you gaze?
"There is no God, we return to sod";
    Surely, he must be crazed.

Of course we must believe in God,
    But is it as far as we go?
Can He not send deliverance then?
    He caused the stars, you know.

Life goes on until He calls,
    Though some are nature's own.
Who can't enjoy these wondrous things
    When they are all alone?

It seems to us if men love God,
    To nature they will go,
And there commune with all that's good,
    So some one else may know.

Know of the harmonies of life,
    Which God must place in tune;
Perhaps if no heart strings break;
    He may dispel all gloom.

THE END

Many are the thoughts that roam
As again I think of home;
Round the castles which we reared,
Going always the way endeared,
Roaming as two lovers would,
Even now I wish we could—
Truly, they were life's greatest inspiration.

From the tangle of the past,
Even from the thoughts that last,
Rear the moments which we spent;
No more we'll know home's real content.

Days have passed with thou at home,
And 'tis many years since you've gone,
Yet thy spirit seems quite near me here alone.

Ere another verse we add,
Little knew we just how sad
Love was in our home just then;
Each failed to think it all could end;
Never has our baby known of that home.

CPSIA information can be obtained
at www.ICGtesting.com
Printed in the USA
BVHW04*1211180918
527831BV00013B/962/P